I'm an IMMIGRANT too!

Mem Fox

Illustrations by
Ronojoy Ghosh

Beach Lane Books New York London Toronto Sydney New Delhi

For
Ignatius Budiman
Moi Yin Choo
Ronojoy Ghosh
Jürgen Kracht
Girolamo Leppa
Helena Nilsson
Gugu Nyoni
Stephan Renc
Acram Taji
Mahmood Tehrani
Sanjay Sinhal
Henny van den Wildenberg
and Lorna Williams—
and also to Stephanie Dowrick,
with great gratitude

—M.F.

For Niharika and Shay,
my favorite Australians

—R.G.

BEACH LANE BOOKS • An imprint of Simon & Schuster Children's Publishing Division • 1230 Avenue of the Americas, New York, New York 10020 • Text copyright © 2017 by Mem Fox • Illustrations copyright © 2017 by Ronojoy Ghosh • Indigenous flag copyright © by Harold Thomas • Originally published in Australia in 2017 by Scholastic Australia as *I'm Australian Too* • 1st US edition 2018 • All rights reserved, including the right of reproduction in whole or in part in any form. • BEACH LANE BOOKS is a trademark of Simon & Schuster, Inc. • For information about special discounts for bulk purchases, please contact Simon & Schuster Special Sales at 1-866-506-1949 or business@simonandschuster.com. • The Simon & Schuster Speakers Bureau can bring authors to your live event. For more information or to book an event, contact the Simon & Schuster Speakers Bureau at 1-866-248-3049 or visit our website at www.simonspeakers.com. • The text for this book was set in YWFT Merriam. • Manufactured in China • 0818 SCP • 10 9 8 7 6 5 4 3 2 1 • Library of Congress Cataloging-in-Publication Data • Names: Fox, Mem, 1946- author. • Title: I'm an immigrant too! / Mem Fox ; illustrated by Ronojoy Ghosh. • Other titles: I am an immigrant too! • Description: First edition. | New York : Beach Lane Books, [2018] | "First published by Scholastic Australia Pty Limited in 2017." | Summary: Illustrations and simple, rhyming text reveal how all of our lives are enriched by the vibrant cultural diversity immigrants bring to their new communities. • Identifiers: LCCN 2018016828 | ISBN 9781534436022 (hardback) • Subjects: | CYAC: Stories in rhyme. | Immigrants—Fiction. | Cultural pluralism—Fiction. | Australia—Fiction. | BISAC: JUVENILE FICTION / Social Issues / Emigration & Immigration. | JUVENILE FICTION / People & Places / Australia & Oceania. | JUVENILE FICTION / Family / General (see also headings under Social Issues). • Classification: LCC PZ8.3.F8245 Iah 2018 | DDC [E]—dc23 LC record available at https://lccn.loc.gov/2018016828

I'm Australian!
How about you?

I'm Australian too!

My mum was born in Sydney,
my dad in Ballarat,
and I was born in Melbourne—
how Australian is that!

My dad grew up in Darwin,
my mum in Humpty Doo.
Our mob's been here forever—
now we share the place with you.

My family came from Ireland
back in 1849.
A million hungry people died,
but now we're doing fine.

My nonno came from Italy—
his family followed after.
At first their lives were very hard,
but now they're full of laughter.

My auntie came from Athens
with her brother and her niece.
And now we live in Adelaide
because it's so like Greece.

My granny came from England
and was homesick every day.
Then she fell in love with Perth,
and now we're here to stay.

Lebanon is beautiful—
my family came from there.
They fled a war, but now they sing:
"Advance Australia Fair"!

I speak just like an Aussie—
which is really who I am!

My family lives in Melbourne,
but we hail from Vietnam.

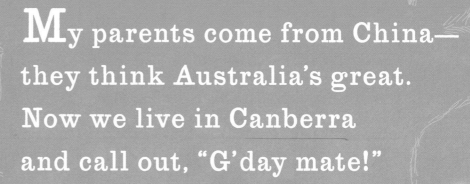

My parents come from China—
they think Australia's great.
Now we live in Canberra
and call out, "G'day mate!"

Somalia was once our home,
but it was torn by strife.
We're happy now in Hobart,
where we have a better life.

My country was Afghanistan—
we fled when I was small.
Our boat capsized, but we were saved—
now we're Australians all.

Syria was where I lived,
but then we had to flee.
Our family's now in Brisbane,
and we're as safe as safe can be.

Sadly, I'm a refugee—
I'm not Australian yet.
But if your country lets me in,
I'd love to be a vet.

We open doors to strangers.
Yes, everyone's a friend.
Australia Fair is ours to share,
where broken hearts can mend.

What journeys we have traveled,
from countries near and far!
Together now, we live in peace,
beneath the Southern Star.

WHERE WE LIVE NOW

PACIFIC
OCEAN

INDIAN
OCEAN

DARWIN

HUMPTY
DOO

GREAT
BARRIER
REEF

AUSTRALIA

BRISBANE

SYDNEY

PERTH

ADELAIDE   BALLARAT   CANBERRA

MELBOURNE

SOUTHERN
OCEAN

HOBART

NEW
ZEALAND